# VINCENT'S SUNFLOWERS

CASSANDRA GAISFORD

# ABOUT THIS BOOK

*Vincent's Sunflowers: A Tale of Love, Light and Legacy*

An extraordinary masterpiece. A world torn by darkness. And the lives forever changed by a field of gold.

From the golden hues of Vincent van Gogh's Sunflowers in a small studio in Arles to the hushed attic of a Jewish family during World War II, to a modern gallery in Tokyo, this sweeping historical fiction explores the enduring power of art to connect, inspire, and heal.

In **1888**, Vincent van Gogh pours his fragile hope and fiery passion into Sunflowers, a hymn to life and light, even as his personal struggles threaten to consume him.

In **1942**, Jakob Rosenfeld, a Jewish art dealer in Nazi-occupied Amsterdam, risks everything to hide the painting, turning his family's attic into a sanctuary for beauty in a time of terror.

In **present-day Tokyo**, curator Hana Mori uncovers the painting's incredible journey, revealing the sacrifices of those who protected it and the secrets it holds for future generations.

Interwoven with historical and personal stories, *Vincent's Sunflowers: A Tale of Love, Light and Legacy* is a heart-stirring novel about resilience, hope, and the unbreakable bonds that art forges across time and humanity.

Perfect for fans of Susan Vreeland and Kristin Hannah, this unforgettable tale will leave you inspired to find light, even in the darkest moments.

# PROLOGUE

"*L*ight in the Darkness"

The little girl's face was a mirror of pure wonder. She stood before the painting, her hands clutching the hem of her grandmother's coat, her gaze fixed on the golden blooms bursting from the canvas. The flowers seemed to stretch beyond their wooden frame, as if they might tumble into the gallery's hushed air and scatter their bright petals across the polished floor. The museum's fluorescent lights tried to compete with the yellows—lemon, ochre, flax—but they couldn't. The colors radiated something more than light: life.

Her grandmother's voice was soft but steady, like the opening notes of an old hymn. "Do you see, Hana? How it shines, even after all it's been through?"

The girl tilted her head, her dark bangs framing her face. "It's just flowers, Obaachan. How can they shine?"

"Ah, but they're not just flowers," the grandmother said, kneeling beside her. Her eyes, lined with years of laughter and sorrow, lingered on the painting as though she were looking at an old friend. "These sunflowers have lived many lives, like people do. And each life has left its mark."

"Like scars?" Hana asked, her finger tracing the jagged edge of the frame without touching it.

"Yes," her grandmother replied. "But also love. And courage. This painting has survived war, darkness, even a little madness. And yet, it shines. Do you know why?"

Hana shook her head, her small brow furrowed in thought.

"Because the artist," her grandmother continued, "believed in the light even when he couldn't see it himself. He painted these flowers not for what they are, but for what they meant to him. To bring light into the world. To make others see it too."

Hana looked up at her grandmother, her wide eyes reflecting the golden hues of the canvas. "Did it work?"

The grandmother's smile was faint, almost wistful. "For some, yes. For others, not yet. But maybe one day, it will."

The girl turned back to the painting, her small frame dwarfed by the bold strokes and radiant yellows. The silence of the gallery settled over them like a quilt, warm and protective. Hana didn't notice the other visitors passing by, nor the distant hum of the air conditioning. She was too busy imagining the story behind the paint—who had touched it, who had seen it, and who had been brave enough to keep it safe.

She didn't yet know that the story of Sunflowers would become part of her own, that the light spilling from the canvas would find its way into her life, even when shadows threatened to overwhelm her.

For now, she only saw flowers. But in time, she would come to see so much more.

# 1

Arles, 1888

The small studio hummed with the frenetic energy of its occupant. Vincent van Gogh leaned close to the canvas, his breath shallow, his hand trembling slightly as it hovered over the surface. The bristles of his brush dipped into a bold yellow mixture, thick as cream, and he swept it across the canvas with deliberate fervor. He paused, tilting his head as though the flowers might whisper to him. He added a touch of white to the yellow—a flash of light—then stepped back, his boots scuffing against the uneven floor.

"Not perfect," he muttered, running a hand through his coppery hair, now streaked with specks of dried paint. "But what is?"

The sunflowers leapt from the canvas, their golden heads bursting with vitality. Some were upright, full of life, while others sagged, their petals curling as if weary from holding the sun. Vincent smiled faintly, his lips barely curving. The flowers weren't just blooms. They were a hymn, a declaration of hope and beauty, a cry against the relentless shadows creeping at the edges of his mind.

The room itself was bare except for his easel, a simple chair, and a cot pressed against the far wall. It was his workshop, his sanctuary, and now, he imagined, the site of an artistic revolution. Paul Gauguin, the master from Paris, would arrive any day now. Together, they would turn this studio in Arles into the "Studio of the South," a haven for kindred spirits who painted not just what they saw, but what they felt.

He closed his eyes and pictured it: Gauguin sitting at this very table, smoking his pipe and discussing color, light, and the untamed passions of art. Vincent would show him the sunflowers —his sunflowers—and they would speak not of technique but of life itself. He needed Gauguin's approval, more than he cared to admit. If only Gauguin could see his work, Vincent thought, he might understand him in a way no one else ever had.

But doubt gnawed at the edges of his vision. He opened his eyes abruptly and turned to the wall where a dozen finished paintings leaned in a precarious line. Each one held a piece of him—a slice of his soul made visible. Still, there was always a whisper in his mind, a voice that told him it wasn't enough. That he wasn't enough.

"Bah!" he barked aloud, startling himself. "Enough of this madness!"

He dipped his brush into a fiery orange, dragging the color boldly across the canvas to deepen the center of a bloom. The light in the room dimmed as the afternoon gave way to evening, but Vincent barely noticed. He painted until the last sliver of daylight disappeared, his strokes feverish, his breathing uneven. Only when his wrist ached did he stop, letting the brush fall into a jar of murky water.

The room was quiet now, except for the distant chatter of neighbors on the street below. He lit a single candle and placed it near the painting. Its soft glow illuminated the sunflowers, casting their golden yellows in an otherworldly light. Vincent studied them with a mixture of pride and sorrow. They were alive, but he felt drained—like he'd given them all the vitality he had left.

In the quiet, the doubts crept back in. Would Gauguin see the light he'd tried to capture? Would he see the madness too? Vincent rubbed his hands together and paced the room. His thoughts spiraled as they always did at night, when the silence became too loud.

But the sunflowers stood firm. Bright. Bold. Resilient. They reminded him of the light he so desperately sought. A flicker of determination stirred in his chest. Gauguin would come. And when he did, Vincent would show him the sunflowers. Whether Gauguin admired them or scoffed, they would stand as a testament to what Vincent believed: art could save even the most fractured soul.

He extinguished the candle and sank onto his cot, his eyes still lingering on the canvas in the darkness. Tomorrow, he would paint more. Tomorrow, he would fill the room with light.

Tomorrow, perhaps, Gauguin would see.

## 2

The laundress arrived early that morning, her arms laden with a basket of clean linens. Rachel's slight figure moved easily through the narrow doorway, her steps light despite the weight of the load. She had the kind of beauty that went unnoticed until it lingered—a softness to her features, framed by loose tendrils of dark hair, and eyes that carried both kindness and a shadow of weariness.

Vincent looked up from his easel as she entered, his brush pausing mid-stroke. "Ah, Rachel," he said, his voice rough from a morning spent muttering to himself. "Come in, come in. Don't mind the mess."

She smiled faintly, accustomed to the chaos of his studio. Paint-smeared rags littered the floor, empty coffee cups lined the windowsill, and unfinished canvases leaned precariously against every available wall. The room smelled of turpentine, oil paint, and the faint, earthy scent of Vincent himself.

"Always the same," she said lightly, setting the basket down on a battered chair. "You'd think an artist might be better at keeping his surroundings beautiful."

He chuckled, a sound that was more rasp than laughter.

"Beauty's meant for the canvas, not the floor." He gestured to the painting before him—a study of sunflowers, their golden petals alive with color.

Rachel stepped closer, wiping her hands on her apron. "They're beautiful," she said simply, tilting her head to take in the vibrant blooms.

"Beautiful," Vincent echoed, his gaze fixed on the flowers. "That's what they should be, isn't it? A light for the weary. A joy for the lost. Even in their decay, there's something... eternal about them."

Rachel glanced at him, her brow furrowing. There was a fragility to him this morning—a restless energy in his move-ments, as if his thoughts were too loud to contain. "You don't sleep much, do you?"

He shrugged, his shoulders tense. "The nights are quiet, but my mind isn't." He stepped back from the canvas and turned to her, his eyes sharp and searching. "Do you ever think about what it means to create something that lasts? Something that matters?"

Rachel hesitated. "I don't know if I've ever had the luxury to think about it."

"Ah," Vincent said, nodding. "Yes, you work with your hands, like me, but in different ways. Washing, mending, stitching lives back together. That matters too, you know. Even if no one sees it."

She felt a warmth rise in her cheeks, surprised by his words. "You give me too much credit."

He waved her modesty away and began pacing the room. "I want this studio, this Studio of the South, to be a place where creation flourishes. Where people like Gauguin and me—people who see the world differently—can work together, challenge each other. Build something larger than ourselves."

Rachel listened, her hands absently smoothing the linens she'd brought. She'd heard about his plans before, but this morn-ing, his voice carried a fervor that made her chest tighten.

"But what if it doesn't work?" she asked, her voice soft.

Vincent stopped pacing and looked at her, his eyes alight with something that could have been hope—or desperation. "Then at least I'll know I tried."

She wanted to tell him that it was enough, that his paintings already spoke louder than words. But she couldn't bring herself to say it. She only nodded, returning her attention to the linens as he resumed his work.

Rachel didn't fully understand Vincent's world of colors and visions, but she understood something deeper—his loneliness, his need to be seen, to matter. And though she couldn't carry his burdens, she could lighten them, if only for a moment.

As she left the studio, her basket empty and her heart unexpectedly heavy, she glanced back at him. He was already lost in his painting again, the world beyond his canvas forgotten.

Rachel smiled faintly and closed the door behind her.

For all his brilliance, Vincent van Gogh was just a man—one who carried the weight of his dreams like a flame in the wind.

# 3

The scent of turpentine hung heavy in the air as Vincent paced the cramped studio, his boots thudding on the scuffed wooden floor. The sunflowers—his beloved sunflowers—stared back at him from the canvas, their golden hues as vivid as the Provençal sun. He had painted them with passion, with purpose, yet now they seemed smaller, dimmer.

Paul Gauguin sat across the room, leaning back in a rickety chair with a cigarette dangling from his lips. His eyes, sharp and calculating, scanned the paintings stacked along the walls. Finally, he exhaled a plume of smoke and turned toward Vincent.

"They're… quaint," Gauguin said, his voice tinged with condescension.

Vincent froze mid-step. "Quaint?" he echoed, his tone incredulous.

Gauguin shrugged, a nonchalant wave of his hand. "Yes. Childish, even. Too much yellow. It overwhelms the eye, drowns the subject. There's no subtlety, no depth."

Vincent's face darkened. His hand clenched the edge of the easel, his knuckles whitening. "Too much yellow?" he said, his voice rising. "These are sunflowers, Paul. They're meant to be yellow—vibrant, alive, reaching for the light!"

"Alive?" Gauguin scoffed, tapping ash into a chipped saucer. "They look like something from a nursery. You should focus on stronger compositions, bolder themes. This... sentimentality doesn't suit you."

The words struck Vincent like a slap. His breath quickened, his thoughts racing. How could Gauguin not see the light, the life, the truth in the sunflowers? He had painted them with his soul, poured every ounce of himself into capturing their essence.

"They're not sentimental," Vincent said through gritted teeth. "They're honest."

"Honest," Gauguin repeated, the word rolling off his tongue like a dismissal. "Honesty is overrated, Vincent. Art should be provocative, transformative, not... this." He gestured vaguely toward the canvas.

Vincent's hand twitched toward a palette knife, not to use it but to feel its weight, its edge. His thoughts spiraled, a torrent of anger and doubt. Was Gauguin right? Had he failed to convey the brilliance he saw so clearly in his mind's eye?

But then his gaze returned to the sunflowers. They stood defiant on the canvas, their petals blazing like fire. They were imperfect, yes, but they were alive. They were his.

"You don't understand," Vincent said, his voice trembling. "You've never understood. These flowers—they're more than objects. They're a celebration, a hymn to the sun, to life itself! You see nursery art, but I see salvation!"

Gauguin's expression turned cold, his patience thinning. "Salvation won't pay your rent, Vincent. It won't put food on the table. You'd do well to think about your audience—what they want, not what you want."

Vincent's temper snapped. "My audience? My audience?" He flung the palette across the room, paint splattering like blood against the wall. "I paint for the light! For those who seek it, who need it! Not for critics or coin or people like you, who look but do not see!"

The outburst hung in the air, sharp and heavy. Gauguin rose slowly, brushing a speck of ash from his lapel. "You're unwell, Vincent," he said, his tone measured but cutting. "This… obsession of yours—it will destroy you."

Vincent laughed bitterly, his hands trembling. "Perhaps," he said, "but I'd rather be destroyed by my passion than live untouched by it."

Gauguin stared at him for a long moment, then turned and walked toward the door. "Suit yourself," he said, pausing briefly in the doorway. "But don't expect anyone else to see the world as you do."

The door slammed shut, leaving Vincent alone with his sunflowers. His chest heaved, his pulse pounding in his ears. The room seemed to close in around him, the shadows growing darker, heavier.

He turned back to the canvas, his vision blurred by unshed tears. The sunflowers stared back, silent but unyielding. They didn't care about Gauguin or his criticisms. They were what they were—bright, bold, and unapologetically alive.

Vincent sank to the floor, his back against the wall, and buried his face in his hands. He was unraveling, piece by piece, but he couldn't stop. He wouldn't stop.

For the light still called to him, even in the darkness.

**4**

---

$\mathcal{T}$he studio was quiet save for the sound of a brush scraping against the canvas. Vincent stood at his easel, his movements feverish, as though trying to outrun the storm gathering in his mind. Sunflowers once more took shape beneath his hands, their petals ablaze with life. But the strokes were harsher now, jagged and uneven, as if the tension in the room had seeped into the paint itself.

Behind him, Paul Gauguin watched, his arms crossed. The cigarette between his fingers smoldered, a thin wisp of smoke curling into the air. He hadn't spoken for several minutes, but his presence was palpable, pressing down on Vincent like a weight.

"You're wasting your talent," Gauguin said finally, his voice cutting through the silence.

Vincent froze, the brush poised in mid-air. Slowly, he turned to face Gauguin, his eyes wide and bloodshot. "Wasting?" he repeated, the word heavy with disbelief. "How dare you—"

"How dare I?" Gauguin interrupted, his tone icy. "You paint the same thing over and over. Flowers, fields, the sun. It's indulgent, Vincent. Obsessive. There's no growth, no evolution."

"No evolution?" Vincent's voice cracked with incredulity. He slammed the brush onto the table, paint splattering across the surface. "Do you know what it takes to capture light, Paul? To make it breathe? To make it live?"

Gauguin took a step forward, his expression hard. "Light won't save you, Vincent. Neither will these sunflowers. You think the world cares about your visions, your endless yellows? They'll forget you the moment you're gone."

Vincent flinched as though struck, his hand gripping the edge of the table for support. His chest heaved, his breath coming in shallow gasps. "You… you think I don't know that?" he whispered. "Do you think I don't feel it every day, every hour? The weight of it? The futility?"

"Then stop!" Gauguin barked, his patience snapping. "Stop this madness and paint something that matters. Something that people will pay for, respect, understand."

The words hit Vincent like a hammer, shattering the fragile equilibrium he'd been clinging to. His mind spiraled, a whirlwind of anger, despair, and the crushing certainty that he would never be enough—not for Gauguin, not for the world, not even for himself.

"You don't understand," Vincent said, his voice trembling with rage. "You've never understood. You're blind, Paul. Blind to the beauty that exists outside your narrow, selfish vision."

"And you," Gauguin shot back, "are a fool chasing shadows. You'll destroy yourself, Vincent, and for what? A canvas no one will care about?"

The silence that followed was electric, thick with the unspoken. Vincent's hands trembled at his sides, his breath coming in ragged bursts.

Then, suddenly, he moved. He grabbed the palette knife from the table and turned it over in his hands, the blade catching the dim light of the room. Gauguin tensed, his eyes narrowing.

"What are you doing, Vincent?" he said cautiously, taking a step back.

But Vincent didn't answer. His thoughts were a cacophony, drowning out everything else. Gauguin's voice, his doubts, his failures—they all blurred together, a relentless tide that threatened to consume him.

In a single, frantic motion, Vincent pressed the knife to his ear. The pain was immediate, searing, but it was nothing compared to the agony in his mind. The room spun, his vision dimming at the edges as blood seeped between his fingers.

"Vincent!" Gauguin's shout cut through the haze, sharp and panicked. He lunged forward, grabbing Vincent by the shoulders and forcing him to sit.

"What have you done?" Gauguin demanded, his voice trembling with a mixture of anger and horror.

But Vincent didn't answer. His gaze was distant, unfocused, as though he were somewhere else entirely.

Rachel appeared in the doorway, her basket slipping from her hands as she took in the scene. "Oh, my God," she whispered, rushing to Vincent's side. She tore a strip of linen from her apron and pressed it to his ear, her hands shaking.

"Stay still," she said, her voice firm despite the tears streaming down her face. "You're going to be all right."

Gauguin turned away, his expression unreadable. He grabbed his coat and left without a word, the door slamming shut behind him.

Rachel stayed, her hands steadying Vincent as his blood mingled with the paint on the floor.

"You're not alone, Vincent," she murmured, though she wasn't sure he could hear her. "You're not alone."

But in that moment, Vincent felt as though he were.

Utterly alone, except for the sunflowers staring back at him from the canvas, their golden heads bowed in silent witness to his pain.

# 5

Amsterdam, 1942

The air in Jakob Rosenfeld's gallery was thick with tension. It wasn't the usual hum of patrons debating the merits of an impressionist landscape or a Baroque still life. No, this was the kind of silence that settled before disaster. Outside, boots stomped down cobblestone streets, their echo a warning.

Jakob stood before Sunflowers, the painting bathed in the pale morning light streaming through the window. Its golden hues seemed defiant, a burst of life in a world steadily growing darker. The Nazis were coming. He had heard it from a fellow dealer, a whispered warning over coffee: "They're cataloging everything. Confiscating anything they deem worthy."

Worthy. Jakob scoffed at the word. What did the Nazis know of worth? To them, art was a trophy, a weapon of propaganda. But to Jakob, Sunflowers was something far greater—a testament to the resilience of the human spirit, to beauty that persisted despite the world's cruelty.

He reached out, his fingers hovering over the canvas's edge. "You've survived so much already," he murmured, as though speaking to the painting itself. "You'll survive this, too."

Behind him, his wife, Miriam, appeared in the doorway, her face drawn with worry. "Jakob, they'll be here soon. You must hurry."

He nodded, forcing his hands to steady as he lifted the painting from the wall. It felt heavier than he remembered, though he knew the weight was not in the frame but in his heart.

Together, they carried Sunflowers up the narrow staircase to the attic. The space smelled of dust and cedar, the air thick and stifling. Jakob knelt beside a loose floorboard, prying it up to reveal a hollow compartment he had prepared weeks ago.

Miriam watched him, her hands clasped tightly. "Will it be safe there?" she asked, her voice trembling.

"As safe as anything can be," he replied. He placed the painting inside with a reverence usually reserved for sacred relics. For Jakob, it was no less than that—a fragment of light in an ever-darkening world.

When the floorboard was replaced and the attic restored to its usual disarray, Jakob leaned back against the wall, his breath coming in shallow gasps. Miriam knelt beside him, placing a hand on his arm.

"What if they find it?" she whispered.

"They won't," he said, though he wasn't sure if he believed it. "And if they do... I'll tell them it was lost, stolen years ago. They'll have no reason to search."

Miriam's eyes filled with tears, but she nodded. They both knew the risks. The Nazis weren't known for their leniency, especially not with men like Jakob—a Jew, an art dealer, a protector of what they sought to destroy.

The sound of boots grew louder, closer. Jakob stood,

brushing off his trousers and forcing a calm he did not feel. "Go downstairs," he told Miriam. "I'll handle this."

She hesitated, her gaze searching his face. "Be careful," she said finally, then disappeared down the staircase.

Jakob descended moments later, straightening his tie as he entered the gallery. Two officers stood in the center of the room, their uniforms immaculate, their expressions cold.

"Jakob Rosenfeld?" one of them asked, his voice clipped.

"Yes," Jakob replied, inclining his head.

"We're here to inspect your collection," the officer continued. "You've been ordered to surrender any works of significant cultural value."

Jakob gestured to the paintings still hanging on the walls, the ones he had deemed less important. "Of course, gentlemen. Take whatever you wish."

The officers moved through the gallery, their eyes scanning each piece with a practiced indifference. Jakob stood by, his heart pounding as one of them paused before an empty spot on the wall where Sunflowers had once hung.

"What was here?" the officer asked, pointing to the bare space.

Jakob's breath caught, but he forced himself to smile. "A modest landscape," he said. "It sold last month to a private collector in Switzerland."

The officer studied him for a moment, then shrugged and moved on.

When the inspection was over, the officers left, carrying several paintings with them. Jakob watched them go, his hands shaking with relief. Miriam appeared at his side, her eyes wide.

"They didn't find it," she said, barely above a whisper.

"No," Jakob replied, though he knew their reprieve was temporary. The war would rage on, and the danger would only grow.

But for now, Sunflowers was safe, hidden in the attic above

their heads. Jakob looked up toward the ceiling, imagining the golden blooms glowing in the dark.

Art could not stop bullets or bombs, but it could endure. It could remind people of what was worth fighting for.

And as long as Jakob lived, he would ensure that this piece of beauty, this fragment of Vincent's vision, would survive.

**6**

---

*T*he boots came at dawn.

I woke to the sound of shouting, loud and harsh, like the barking of wolves. Papa had warned us this day might come, but nothing could prepare me for the way it felt—the air thick with fear, the pounding on the door reverberating through the walls.

"Miriam, take Lea upstairs," Papa said, his voice steady despite the panic in his eyes. He was already dressed, his tie perfectly knotted, as if the officers at the door were simply guests at the gallery.

Mama's hand trembled as she gripped mine, pulling me toward the staircase. I didn't want to go. I wanted to stay, to stand beside Papa, to tell those men they couldn't take what was ours. But I was thirteen, and what could a thirteen-year-old girl do against Nazis with guns?

In the attic, Mama whispered for me to be quiet, her arms wrapped around me like a shield. The air was cold, and I could hear every creak of the floorboards below as Papa led the officers into the gallery.

"This is my collection," he said, his voice carrying up through the wooden beams. "You may take what you wish."

I bit my lip to keep from crying as I imagined them tearing the paintings from the walls, their hands rough and careless. But when I thought of Sunflowers, hidden beneath the floorboards just feet away, my heart clenched. If they found it, everything Papa had done—his lies, his risks—would mean nothing.

One of the officers must have asked about the empty space on the wall, because I heard Papa's reply: "It sold last month to a collector in Switzerland." His tone was calm, almost bored, but I knew better. I knew how much he loved that painting, how many nights he had spent staring at it as though it might offer him answers.

The shouting stopped after what felt like hours but must have only been minutes. Mama's grip on me tightened as footsteps echoed on the staircase. The officers were coming closer.

I held my breath as the attic door creaked open. Mama pressed a finger to her lips, her eyes wide with terror.

"Just storage," Papa's voice said from the doorway, firm but casual. "Old furniture, broken frames. Nothing of interest."

The footsteps stopped, then retreated. The attic door slammed shut.

I didn't exhale until the front door below opened and closed again, the sound of boots fading into the distance.

**December 9, 1942**

Papa stayed up late last night, long after the officers had gone. I watched him from the top of the stairs, a shadow against the dim light of the gallery. He stood where Sunflowers used to hang, his hands clasped behind his back, his head bowed.

When I asked him why he had risked everything to save that painting, he didn't answer right away.

Finally, he said, "Because some things are worth more than safety. More than life itself."

I don't fully understand what he means, but I think it has to do with hope. Papa always says that art reminds us of what the world could be, not just what it is. That it shows us beauty even in the midst of darkness.

When I look at Sunflowers, I think of light. Not just the yellow of the flowers, but the kind of light that makes you feel warm inside, that makes you believe things will get better, even when everything seems lost.

Papa says we're fighting to save more than paintings. We're fighting to save the soul of the world.

I hope we can.

## 7

*K*laus Adler stepped into the Rosenfeld gallery, his boots echoing sharply against the wooden floor. His gaze swept the room, cataloging every detail—the ornate frames, the muted landscapes, the still-life vases. Yet, something lingered in the air here, something unspoken, as though the walls themselves were holding their breath.

Jakob Rosenfeld stood by the window, his hands clasped tightly behind his back, his face calm but pale. Klaus had been trained to recognize fear. It was in the slight tremor of the man's hands, the way his eyes flickered toward the staircase before he caught himself.

"Your collection," Klaus said curtly, gesturing to the walls. "Show me."

Jakob inclined his head. "Of course, Herr Adler."

He walked slowly, deliberately, through the gallery, pointing out each piece with the practiced air of a seasoned art dealer. Klaus followed, nodding absently as Jakob described the origins of a Flemish landscape, the technique of a Parisian still life. But it was a charade—one Klaus had seen many times before. The real treasure was always hidden.

Klaus paused in front of a bare spot on the wall, its edges faintly darker where a frame had once hung. He turned to Jakob. "What was here?"

Jakob hesitated, just for a moment, but long enough for Klaus to notice. "A modest work," Jakob said. "Sold recently to a collector in Switzerland."

"Convenient," Klaus remarked, stepping closer. "And this collector—do you have their name? Their address?"

"I'm afraid not," Jakob replied, his voice steady despite the tension in his posture. "The sale was handled through an intermediary."

Klaus studied him, his sharp blue eyes narrowing. He could feel the lie, the way it lingered in the air like a faint scent. But then something shifted. His gaze caught on a staircase at the back of the room, leading upward.

Without a word, he started toward it. Jakob's face tightened, his mouth opening as if to protest, but he said nothing.

The attic was small and cluttered, filled with dusty crates and forgotten furniture. Klaus stepped inside, his boots stirring up small clouds of dust. The air was colder here, heavier.

He moved slowly, his gloved hand brushing against a crate, the corner of a table, as though searching for something he couldn't name. Then he saw it—a floorboard, slightly raised at the edge, almost imperceptible.

He knelt, his fingers tracing the seam. With a quick motion, he lifted the board, revealing the hollow space beneath. And there it was.

Sunflowers.

The colors were brighter than he'd imagined, even in the dim light of the attic. The yellows glowed, vibrant and alive, as though the flowers had been plucked from a field only moments ago. Klaus stared at the painting, his breath catching.

For a long moment, he forgot where he was, forgot the war, the uniform he wore. All he could see was the light—the light

Vincent van Gogh had captured with every furious stroke of his brush.

Jakob's voice broke the spell. "Please," he said softly, standing in the doorway. "Let it stay. It's not just a painting. It's… it's everything."

Klaus looked up at him, the man's thin frame silhouetted against the dim light from the stairs. His words were desperate, but there was something else in his eyes—conviction.

"You risk your life for this?" Klaus asked, his voice low.

Jakob nodded. "Not just mine. My family's. And I'd do it again. Because some things are worth the risk."

Klaus turned back to the painting. He knew the orders. Any valuable art was to be confiscated, shipped back to Germany for the Reich's glory. Defiance meant punishment—imprisonment, even execution.

But as he stared at Sunflowers, something inside him shifted. He thought of his own father, a painter who had abandoned his brushes when the war came. Of the afternoons he'd spent as a boy in his father's studio, watching him bring light and shadow to life.

This painting wasn't just pigment on canvas. It was something more. Something pure.

Klaus stood, replacing the floorboard with deliberate care. He turned to Jakob, his face unreadable.

"I saw nothing," he said quietly. "Do you understand?"

Jakob's breath hitched, but he nodded. "Yes. Thank you."

Without another word, Klaus descended the stairs, his heart pounding. He knew the risks, knew what it would mean if his superiors discovered his act of mercy. But as he stepped out into the cold street, the image of those sunflowers stayed with him, their brightness seared into his mind.

Sometimes, even in war, light found a way to survive.

## 8

---

he night was silent, heavy with the weight of secrets. Jakob Rosenfeld adjusted the straps of the canvas bag slung over his shoulder, his fingers trembling as he fastened the latch. Every sound—the creak of the floorboards, the rustle of Lea's coat—felt amplified in the stillness.

"We'll go out the back," Jakob whispered, his voice barely audible. "Keep close to me. Don't look back."

Lea nodded, clutching the small satchel that held the few belongings they could carry. Her wide eyes betrayed her fear, but she didn't cry. At fourteen, she had learned that tears wouldn't save them.

Miriam stood by the doorway, her face pale, her hands gripping the edges of her shawl. "Are you certain about this?" she asked, her voice wavering.

Jakob met her gaze, his expression both resolute and haunted. "They're coming, Miriam. It's only a matter of time. If we stay…" He didn't finish the sentence. He didn't need to.

Lea stepped forward, tugging at her mother's sleeve. "You'll follow us soon, won't you?" she asked, her voice small.

Miriam forced a smile, brushing a strand of hair from her

daughter's face. "Of course, mein Schatz. It's only for a little while. You'll see."

But they all knew the truth.

Jakob's eyes flicked upward, toward the attic where Sunflowers lay hidden beneath the floorboards. He had spent days wrestling with the decision, weighing the risk of taking the painting against the certainty of their own survival. In the end, the choice had been made for him.

"Leave it," Miriam had said, her voice firm despite the tears in her eyes. "The world needs it more than we do. We'll come back for it. One day."

Now, as they prepared to leave, Jakob felt the weight of the loss as keenly as if he were leaving a part of himself behind. But Miriam was right. The painting was more than a possession. It was a beacon, a promise of light in the darkness. And for that, it had to stay.

"Let's go," Jakob said, his voice tight.

They slipped out the back door, the cold night air biting at their faces. The streets of Amsterdam were eerily quiet, the usual hum of life replaced by the distant hum of military vehicles.

Jakob led the way, his eyes scanning the shadows for any sign of movement. Lea followed close behind, her small hand clutching his coat.

As they crossed the canal, the sound of boots on cobble-stones made them freeze. Jakob pushed Lea into the shadow of an alley, his heart pounding. A patrol passed, their voices low, their rifles slung casually over their shoulders.

When the soldiers disappeared around a corner, Jakob exhaled slowly, his grip on Lea's shoulder tightening. "Come," he whispered.

They moved quickly after that, darting through alleyways and slipping through backstreets. Their destination was the home of a sympathetic baker who had agreed to hide them until arrangements could be made for their escape from the city.

When they finally arrived, Jakob knocked softly on the wooden door. It opened almost immediately, revealing a stout man with flour-dusted hands and kind eyes.

"Come in, quickly," the baker said, ushering them inside.

The warmth of the kitchen was a stark contrast to the chill of the night. Jakob sank into a chair, his exhaustion finally catching up with him. Lea clung to his arm, her face buried in his sleeve.

"You'll be safe here for now," the baker said, placing a steaming cup of tea in front of Jakob. "But you must leave soon. The patrols are increasing."

Jakob nodded, his mind already racing with plans. But as the baker spoke, his thoughts drifted back to the attic, to the painting hidden beneath the floorboards. Would it survive? Would anyone ever find it?

"Papa," Lea whispered, tugging at his sleeve. "Do you think they'll find it?"

Jakob looked at her, his throat tightening. "No," he said firmly. "They won't."

But in his heart, he wasn't sure.

That night, as Jakob and Lea lay on makeshift beds in the baker's cellar, the image of Sunflowers filled his mind. He could see its golden blooms glowing in the darkness, a reminder of everything they were fighting to protect.

The painting was no longer his, not truly. It belonged to the world, to the future.

As the first light of dawn crept through the cracks in the cellar door, Jakob whispered a silent prayer—for the painting, for his family, for a world that might one day know peace again.

And then they fled.

## 9

*Tokyo, Present Day*

*H*ana Mori leaned over the display case, the harsh overhead lights reflecting off the glass. Her meticulous hands adjusted the label below the framed photograph of Van Gogh's Sunflowers, her sharp eye catching the smallest tilt in the text. Perfect. Everything had to be perfect.

The upcoming auction was the talk of Tokyo's art world, drawing international collectors and critics to her museum. Van Gogh's Sunflowers was the star attraction—a painting that carried not just beauty but a storied legacy. The museum had partnered with a private seller to bring the piece to market, and Hana had been tasked with ensuring the exhibition showcased its grandeur and historical significance.

She stepped back, taking in the gallery space. The centerpiece, the Sunflowers, stood on a pedestal in the center of the room, encased in climate-controlled glass. Its yellows radiated under the soft lights, as if the painting itself exuded warmth.

"Looks stunning, doesn't it?" said Dr. Emily Carter, an art historian and Hana's colleague. Emily stood by the entrance, a steaming cup of green tea in her hand.

Hana nodded, her lips curving into a small smile. "It's mesmerizing. Every time I look at it, I feel like I'm seeing it for the first time."

"Van Gogh had a way of doing that," Emily said, stepping closer. "But you seem tense. What's on your mind?"

Hana sighed, crossing her arms over her tailored blazer. "It's the provenance. There are gaps in the painting's history during the war years. We have documents from a Dutch collector in the 1930s, but then there's nothing until it reappears in Japan in the late 1940s."

Emily raised an eyebrow. "That's not unusual. Art shifted hands so many times during the war—sold, stolen, or hidden. What's troubling you?"

Hana hesitated. "There's something else. A rumor. One of the researchers mentioned a story about the painting being hidden by a Jewish family in Amsterdam before the war. If that's true..." She trailed off, her mind racing.

"It could complicate the sale," Emily finished, her tone thoughtful. "Or make it more valuable, depending on how the story is spun."

Hana frowned. "I don't care about the sale. I care about the truth. If there's a chance this painting was stolen—or worse—then we have a responsibility to find out."

Emily tilted her head, studying Hana. "You're taking a risk, Hana. Digging into provenance can open doors you might not want to walk through. Are you sure about this?"

Hana's gaze drifted back to the painting, the sunflowers glowing softly in their glass enclosure. "It's not just a painting, Emily. It's a piece of history. If we don't protect its story, who will?"

Emily nodded slowly. "Fair point. Where do you want to

start?"

"I've requested access to additional records from the private seller," Hana said. "But I also want to dig into the archives. If the story about Amsterdam is true, there has to be a clue somewhere."

Emily smirked. "You love a good mystery, don't you?"

Hana allowed herself a brief laugh. "Maybe. Or maybe I'm just stubborn."

The two women stood in silence for a moment, their eyes fixed on the painting. It seemed almost alive, its golden blooms a testament to resilience and light. For Hana, it wasn't enough to marvel at its beauty. She needed to understand it, to uncover the secrets it held.

As the museum began to fill with staff and early visitors, Hana turned to Emily. "I'll be in the archives if you need me."

Emily raised her tea in a mock toast. "Good luck. I have a feeling you're about to uncover something big."

Hana smiled faintly, her heels clicking softly against the marble floor as she walked away. Deep down, she knew Emily was right. This wasn't just another auction. It was the beginning of a journey—one that would lead her to answers she wasn't sure she was ready for.

But she owed it to the painting, to the history it carried, and to the people who had risked everything to save it.

## 10

*H*ana Mori adjusted her scarf as she stepped into the private lounge of Kenji Takahashi's corporate headquarters. The space exuded quiet opulence, with sleek lines, muted tones, and an understated arrangement of rare art on the walls. Hana's gaze lingered briefly on a contemporary sculpture, its angular form an intriguing contrast to the classical pieces she worked with.

Kenji Takahashi greeted her with a polite bow, his tailored suit impeccably pressed. In his mid-fifties, Kenji carried himself with the poised elegance of a man accustomed to commanding attention, though his piercing eyes betrayed an intensity that set him apart from other collectors Hana had encountered.

"Thank you for meeting with me, Mr. Takahashi," Hana began, her tone formal but warm.

"It's my pleasure, Ms. Mori," he replied, gesturing for her to sit. "Anything related to Van Gogh's Sunflowers is of great interest to me."

Hana settled into the leather armchair, her notebook and pen ready. "I understand you've been a patron of the arts for many years, but your particular interest in this painting seems personal. May I ask why?"

Kenji leaned back, his expression softening. "You're perceptive, Ms. Mori. Yes, my interest in Sunflowers is deeply personal. It connects to a story my grandmother used to tell—a story that shaped much of who I am."

Hana leaned forward, her pen poised. "Please, go on."

Kenji's gaze drifted to the large window behind her, where the city skyline stretched into the distance. "My grandmother, Akiko Takahashi, was a young nurse during the post-war recovery. Japan was in ruins, and people were trying to piece their lives back together, both physically and emotionally. She worked in a small hospital in Tokyo, treating patients who had lost everything—their homes, their families, their hope."

He paused, his voice tightening with emotion. "One day, a foreign soldier, part of the Allied forces, brought a painting to the hospital as a gesture of goodwill. It was Sunflowers."

Hana's breath caught. "The Van Gogh? Here, in Tokyo?"

Kenji nodded. "Yes. The soldier said it was meant to bring light into the hospital's wards, to remind the patients that beauty could still exist even amidst destruction."

Hana's mind raced. This was the first she'd heard of the painting's presence in Japan before it entered private collections. "What happened to it?"

Kenji smiled faintly. "It hung in the hospital for a time. My grandmother said she would sit by it during her breaks, staring at those bright yellow blooms. She told me it gave her strength, a kind of hope she couldn't explain. She said it reminded her that even in the darkest moments, something as simple as a sunflower could reach for the sun."

Hana swallowed the lump forming in her throat. "And then?"

"When the hospital closed, the painting disappeared," Kenji continued. "My grandmother never knew where it went. But she spoke of it often, even in her final days. She told me it was a symbol, not just of survival but of renewal."

"That's... incredible," Hana said softly, her voice filled with awe. "And you believe this is the same Sunflowers we have now?"

Kenji met her gaze, his expression unreadable. "I do. And if it's true, then this painting carries a story far greater than we realize. It's not just art. It's a piece of history, a beacon for those who have endured unimaginable loss."

Hana's pen moved across the page, capturing every word. "Thank you for sharing this, Mr. Takahashi. It adds another layer to what we already know about the painting's journey."

Kenji smiled, but his intensity remained. "I only ask one thing, Ms. Mori. If you uncover more about the painting's provenance, especially its time here in Japan, I'd like to know. My grandmother's memory deserves that recognition."

Hana nodded solemnly. "You have my word. I'll do everything I can to uncover the truth."

As she left Kenji's office, Hana felt a renewed sense of purpose. Sunflowers wasn't just a masterpiece. It was a thread connecting lives across generations and continents. And she was determined to ensure its story was told, in all its complexity and light.

*H*ana Mori sat across from Dr. Emily Carter in the dimly lit archive room of the Tokyo Museum of Art. The faint hum of the overhead lights and the rustle of old documents filled the space as they pored over faded records and fragile correspondence. The room smelled of dust and ink, a testament to decades of history waiting to be uncovered.

"Here's something," Emily said, sliding a yellowed ledger toward Hana. "An export record from Amsterdam in late 1945. Look at the consignee."

Hana leaned over, squinting at the faded type. "Takahashi Trading Company," she murmured. "It was Kenji's grandfather's business, wasn't it?"

Emily nodded. "It seems they handled shipments of art and antiques post-war. Some were repatriated to Europe, but others remained here in Japan. This could explain how Sunflowers ended up in Tokyo."

Hana's mind raced. "But why wasn't it officially recorded? If Sunflowers was part of a legitimate transaction, it should have been documented more thoroughly."

"Not necessarily," Emily replied, tapping her pen against the ledger. "This was right after the war. Records were chaotic, and some shipments were deliberately vague to avoid scrutiny—either for financial reasons or to protect items with contested provenance."

Hana frowned, flipping through her notes. "If this ledger is accurate, then the painting was likely shipped from Amsterdam. That would align with Jakob Rosenfeld's story about hiding it during the Nazi occupation."

Emily leaned back, her expression thoughtful. "So, we have a chain forming: hidden in an attic during the war, smuggled to Japan after the war, then brought into private hands. But we're still missing the critical link—how did it survive the Nazi raids?"

Hana tapped her notebook with her pen, her mind tracing the path they'd uncovered so far. "We need to confirm the Amsterdam connection. Jakob's family might still have records —or even someone who remembers the story."

Emily's eyes lit up. "It's worth a shot. I'll reach out to a colleague at the Rijksmuseum who specializes in WWII-era provenance research. Maybe they can help us dig deeper into Rosenfeld's archives."

Hana nodded, her excitement growing. "Meanwhile, I'll reach out to Kenji Takahashi again. His family might have additional documents about the post-war shipments, especially if the painting came through his grandfather's company."

A WEEK LATER, Hana and Emily reconvened in Hana's office, each armed with new findings. Emily spread a series of black-and-white photographs across the desk, each depicting a cluttered attic filled with crates and canvases.

"These came from the Rijksmuseum's WWII archives," Emily explained. "They were taken by Dutch Resistance members documenting stolen and hidden art. Look here."

Hana leaned closer, her heart skipping a beat. In one of the photos, partially visible beneath a tarp, was a canvas unmistakably depicting Sunflowers.

"It's the same painting," Hana whispered. "They hid it under the floorboards, just like Jakob's story said."

Emily nodded. "Jakob Rosenfeld and his family risked everything to protect it. The Nazis came close to finding it, but a sympathetic officer—Klaus Adler—chose to overlook it. His name came up in a post-war trial, but he disappeared before he could be questioned."

Hana let the weight of the discovery settle over her. "So, the painting survived the war because of Jakob's bravery—and a moment of mercy from a man who could have destroyed it."

"But it's not the end of the story," Emily said, pulling out another document. "This is from the Takahashi Trading Company archives. It details a shipment of 'cultural artifacts' from Amsterdam to Tokyo in December 1945. The description is vague, but the dimensions match Sunflowers."

Hana's breath caught. "It's the missing link."


THAT EVENING, Hana sat alone in her office, staring at a print of Sunflowers pinned to her wall. The painting had endured so much—war, loss, and the silent sacrifices of those who had protected it.

Picking up her pen, she began drafting a report, weaving together the fragments of history they had uncovered. This wasn't just about Sunflowers. It was about the people whose lives had been touched by it—the Rosenfelds, Klaus Adler, Akiko Takahashi—and the enduring light that had carried them through the darkness.

The painting wasn't just a masterpiece. It was a testament to resilience, to the beauty that survived when everything else seemed lost.

And now, Hana thought, it was her responsibility to ensure the world knew its story.

## 12

---

The dusty smell of the archives lingered in the air as Hana and Emily combed through box after box of aged documents. Each yellowed page and faded photograph told a story, but none yet revealed the crucial piece they were searching for—the proof that would secure Sunflowers' place in history.

Emily brushed a stray strand of hair from her face, her gloves smudged with specks of grime. "If we don't find anything soon, I might start to believe this letter is a myth," she muttered, half to herself.

Hana, seated across from her, refused to let the fatigue show in her voice. "We'll find it. Letters between Vincent and Theo are rare, but they exist. And if it's here, it will be worth every hour we've spent digging."

Emily sighed but nodded, pulling another folder from a worn cardboard box labeled **Arles, 1888–1889**. Hana had been meticulously documenting every find, even those that seemed irrelevant, convinced that one overlooked detail could hold the key.

It was nearly midnight when Emily let out a sharp intake of breath. "Hana. I think… I think this is it."

Hana looked up sharply, her heart racing as Emily carefully unfolded a fragile piece of parchment. The handwriting, bold and slanted, was unmistakably Van Gogh's.

"Let me see," Hana said, moving closer.

Emily handed her the letter, her hands trembling slightly. "It's addressed to Theo. Look at the date—August 1888."

Hana's eyes scanned the page, the words leaping out at her with every line:

*"My dear Theo,*

*The sunflowers are finished, though I cannot say if they are truly done. Do we ever finish what we set out to do? Yet, they glow with a light I hope will carry beyond my small room, beyond my own fleeting life.*

*These flowers, with their yellows so bright, so alive—they are not merely blooms. They are a prayer. A hymn to the sun, to the warmth it gives, and to the life it sustains. I see in them a kind of eternity, the resilience of beauty in the face of decay.*

*One day, Theo, I hope others will see this too. Perhaps long after I am gone, they will find in these flowers the hope I felt as I painted them. A beacon, yes, for those who need light in their darkness. Let them be my offering, my message to a world I will never know."*

*Your loving brother,*
*Vincent*
*August 1888.*

HANA'S THROAT tightened as she finished reading. "He painted them for hope," she whispered, her voice thick with emotion.

Emily leaned back in her chair, staring at the letter as if it

held the answers to all of life's questions. "This changes everything," she said. "It's not just about the painting anymore. It's
about what it represents—what Vincent wanted it to mean."

Hana nodded, carefully placing the letter back into its protective sleeve. "This proves Sunflowers is authentic, yes. But it also
deepens its legacy. Every person who's seen this painting, who's
drawn strength from it, is connected to that moment in Vincent's
studio. To his dream of bringing light to others."

Emily smiled faintly. "Ironic, isn't it? That a man who strug-
gled so much to find his own light would create something that's
inspired so many."

Hana didn't reply, her mind already racing ahead. This letter
wasn't just a confirmation of authenticity—it was a story. A story
that would captivate the art world, resonate with collectors, and
cement Sunflowers' place as one of the most meaningful works
in history.

But more than that, it was a gift. From Vincent to Theo.
From the past to the present. From the artist to the world.

Hana carefully packed the letter for preservation, her heart
full with the weight of what they had uncovered. She glanced at
Emily, her voice firm but filled with awe. "We need to make this
public. The world deserves to know."

Emily nodded, her expression resolute. "Let's make sure
they do."

## 13

The grand hall of the Tokyo Museum of Art was transformed into a stage for history. Beneath the soaring arches of the ceiling, journalists, art enthusiasts, and dignitaries gathered in anticipation. The air hummed with quiet excitement, the kind that preceded revelations capable of changing how the world saw itself.

Hana Mori stood near the podium, her hands clasped tightly in front of her. She wore her professional calm like armor, but inside, her heart raced. After months of research, sleepless nights in archives, and moments of doubt, the moment had arrived.

To her right, Dr. Emily Carter adjusted her glasses and offered Hana a reassuring smile. "You're going to be brilliant," Emily said softly.

Hana nodded, exhaling slowly. "It's not about me. It's about Sunflowers."

She stepped onto the podium, the murmurs in the audience fading to silence. Behind her, on the stage, Van Gogh's Sunflowers was displayed in its protective glass case, its golden hues glowing under the soft spotlights. The painting seemed to radiate its own warmth, a beacon of light that commanded reverence.

"Good evening," Hana began, her voice steady. "Thank you all for being here to witness a moment of profound significance —not only for the art world but for history itself."

She gestured toward the painting. "Van Gogh's Sunflowers has long been celebrated as a masterpiece. Its vibrant yellows, its bold strokes, its life captured on canvas—these elements have inspired generations. But tonight, we share a story that transcends its beauty. A story of resilience, hope, and the enduring power of light in the face of darkness."

The audience leaned forward, captivated.

"Through our research, we have traced the extraordinary journey of this painting," Hana continued. "From Van Gogh's studio in Arles, where it was created as a hymn to the sun, to an attic in Amsterdam, where it was hidden by a Jewish family during the horrors of World War II."

A collective gasp rippled through the room.

"It was protected at great personal risk by Jakob Rosenfeld, a man who understood that preserving beauty was an act of defiance against oppression. Later, it found its way to Japan, where it became a symbol of renewal for those rebuilding their lives after the devastation of war."

Hana paused, letting the weight of her words settle. "And now, thanks to an extraordinary discovery, we have Vincent's own words—a letter to his brother, Theo, in which he describes Sunflowers as a beacon of hope. His intention was clear: this painting was meant to bring light to those who need it most."

The screen behind her illuminated with an image of the letter, its faded ink a testament to time. Murmurs of astonishment spread through the crowd.

"This is not just a painting," Hana said, her voice rising with conviction. "It is a story of survival, of courage, of the human spirit's capacity to endure. It is a reminder that even in our darkest moments, there is light."

She stepped back, allowing the audience to absorb the painting in its full glory. The room was silent, but it was not the silence of indifference. It was reverence.

Emily joined her at the podium, a proud smile on her face. "You did it," she whispered.

"No," Hana replied, her gaze fixed on the painting. "They did it. Van Gogh, Jakob, Klaus Adler, Akiko Takahashi—they all carried this light forward. We're just the messengers."

As the evening progressed, the story of Sunflowers spread like wildfire, shared in headlines, social media posts, and whispered conversations. The painting, once simply a masterpiece, was now a symbol.

And as Hana watched the crowd, their faces illuminated by the golden hues of Van Gogh's vision, she knew the painting had been reborn—not just as art but as hope.

## 14

*H*ana Mori sat alone in the gallery late that night, the crowd long gone, the museum silent except for the faint hum of the climate-control system. Sunflowers stood in its glass case, the spotlights now dimmed to a soft glow. Without the bustling energy of earlier, the painting seemed quieter, more intimate, as though it waited patiently for the next person to gaze upon it.

She let out a slow breath, her body still buzzing with the adrenaline of the evening's presentation. Her mind, however, was somewhere else. She thought of the letter, its fragile ink spilling Vincent's thoughts across time.

"A beacon, yes, for those who need light in their darkness."

Hana glanced at her notebook, now closed on her lap, and thought of the people connected by this single piece of art. Vincent, pouring his hope and desperation into those golden blooms. Jakob, risking everything to shield it from destruction. Klaus Adler, choosing to turn a blind eye in an act of quiet defiance. Kenji's grandmother, Akiko, drawing strength from its light during the grim days of post-war recovery.

Each life had left a mark on the painting's journey, as though they had all added a stroke to its canvas.

"Art doesn't just reflect the artist," she murmured, her voice barely audible in the empty hall. "It reflects everyone who touches it, everyone who carries it forward."

She stood, walking slowly toward the painting. The yellows glimmered faintly, as if still burning with the passion Vincent had poured into them. She thought of Jakob, shielding it from Nazi confiscation. His daughter, Lea, writing about her father's bravery in her diary. Did they ever imagine that their choices would resonate across decades?

Hana thought of Kenji, whose grandmother had seen the same light Vincent intended, even as she worked to heal a broken nation. And now Kenji himself, honoring her memory by ensuring the painting's story was told.

She reached out, her hand stopping just shy of the glass. "It's not just a painting," she whispered. "It's all of us. Our fears. Our hopes. Our need to believe in something bigger than ourselves."

For a moment, she thought of her own life—how she had dedicated herself to uncovering the truth behind objects others might see as static relics. But now, standing before Sunflowers, she understood that art was alive. It was a thread binding people across time and space, connecting lives in ways that words alone could never achieve.

A faint sound broke her reverie. She turned to see Emily standing in the doorway, holding two steaming cups of tea. "I thought you could use this," Emily said, walking toward her.

Hana accepted the cup with a grateful smile. "Thank you."

Emily took a sip of her tea, her gaze shifting to the painting. "You know, I think this is what Vincent wanted. For his work to mean something, to touch lives long after he was gone."

Hana nodded. "And it has. It's touched more lives than he could have imagined." She paused, her voice growing thoughtful. "Do you think that's what art is meant to do? Carry pieces of us forward, connecting the past to the present?"

Emily smiled. "Absolutely. Art is humanity's way of leaving breadcrumbs for the future. It's how we say, 'We were here, and this is what we felt. This is what mattered to us.'"

Hana took a deep breath, the weight of the evening giving way to a quiet sense of peace. "I think that's what I want to do—to help carry those breadcrumbs forward. To protect them so others can find their way."

They stood in silence, sipping their tea as the painting seemed to watch over them, its golden blooms radiant even in the dim light.

Hana realized then that Sunflowers wasn't just a symbol of resilience or beauty. It was a testament to humanity itself—to the people who had loved, sacrificed, and persevered so that something as fragile as a painting could endure.

And as long as the painting stood, so too would the stories it carried.

## 15

The gallery was quiet, save for the soft hum of murmured voices and the occasional shuffle of footsteps on the polished floor. Light poured through the high windows, diffused and golden, as though nature itself conspired to honor Van Gogh's Sunflowers.

Hana Mori stood at the back of the room, watching the visitors as they gathered around the painting. Schoolchildren in neatly pressed uniforms, their faces filled with wide-eyed wonder. An elderly couple holding hands, their expressions softened by the shared memory of decades past. A lone man in a business suit, his briefcase at his feet, gazing at the painting as if seeing it for the first time.

Each of them drawn to the same thing: the light.

The yellows of the sunflowers blazed, brighter than the sun outside. The strokes of paint seemed alive, carrying with them the fervor and fragility of the artist who had placed them there. Time had not dulled their vibrancy, nor had the trials they endured dimmed their message.

Hana's chest swelled with a quiet pride. This was where

Sunflowers belonged—not hidden away in a private collection or locked behind vault doors, but here, open to the world.

She wandered closer, catching snippets of conversation as she passed.

"Did you know Van Gogh painted this for his friend Gauguin? Imagine what he must have felt creating it," one visitor said to another.

A young boy tugged on his mother's sleeve. "The flowers look like they're glowing," he whispered, his eyes never leaving the canvas.

"They do," his mother replied softly.

Hana stopped a few feet from the painting, her gaze lifting to meet its golden blooms. She had spent so much time uncovering its story—every detail, every life it had touched—but now, she realized, the painting no longer belonged to her. It belonged to everyone who stood before it, to everyone who saw in its vibrant yellows a piece of themselves.

She thought of Vincent, sitting in his small studio in Arles, pouring his hope and anguish into each stroke. Of Jakob, hiding the painting beneath floorboards to save it from destruction. Of Kenji's grandmother, who found solace in its light during her darkest days.

The room swelled with life, each visitor adding their own story to the painting's legacy. Hana felt a sense of completion, not just for her work, but for the painting's journey.

As she turned to leave, her eyes caught on a small girl standing alone before the painting. She couldn't have been more than six or seven, her face illuminated by the soft glow of the sunflowers. The child tilted her head, as though listening to a secret only she could hear.

Hana smiled. "What do you see?" she asked gently.

The girl turned, her dark eyes wide. "It's like they're happy," she said. "Even though it looks like they're old, they're still happy."

Hana felt her throat tighten. "That's exactly right," she said softly.

She walked to the gallery's exit, pausing for a moment to glance back. The painting stood at the center of the room, bathed in light, surrounded by people from all walks of life. It had survived war, loss, and countless challenges, but now, it was more than a painting.

It was a testament to hope. To resilience. To the enduring power of beauty to connect, inspire, and heal.

As Hana stepped into the bright afternoon, she carried with her the knowledge that Sunflowers would continue its work, speaking to generations yet to come, reminding them that even in the darkest moments, there is always light to be found.

# EPILOGUE

*T*he cursor blinked on the screen, steady and unyielding. Hana Mori stared at the blank document for what felt like an eternity, her thoughts swirling. She had spent months uncovering the story of Sunflowers, piecing together the fragments of its journey through time. Now, it was her turn to tell its story—not as a curator or a researcher, but as a person who had been changed by it.

She began typing, her words flowing with the rhythm of her heart:

*There is something about yellow that demands attention. It's the color of the sun, of life, of energy. For Vincent van Gogh, yellow was more than a hue; it was a language. In his painting of sunflowers, he spoke to us across centuries, using the color as a cry against darkness, as a reminder that even the most fragile things—like petals and light—can endure.*

*For me, Sunflowers has become more than a painting. It is a bridge, connecting past to present, light to shadow, despair to hope. Each brushstroke carries with it the story of Vincent, pouring his heart into those blooms in a small room in Arles.*

*But it also carries the stories of those who protected it, believed in it, and found themselves reflected in its vibrant yellows.*

HANA PAUSED, her fingers resting on the keys. She thought of Jakob Rosenfeld and his family, risking their lives to hide the painting from Nazi hands. She imagined his daughter, Lea, writing in her diary about the courage it took to protect beauty in a time of destruction. She pictured Klaus Adler, the conflicted officer who chose mercy over orders, and Kenji's grandmother, Akiko, who found hope in the painting's light during Japan's recovery.

She continued writing:

*Art, at its best, doesn't just exist; it connects. It reminds us that we are part of a larger story, one that transcends our individual lives. For Vincent, those sunflowers were a prayer, a hymn to life. For Jakob, they were an act of defiance. For Akiko, they were strength in a time of rebuilding. And for me, they have become a reminder that light persists, even when it feels like it's fading.*

*In a world that often feels fractured and fragile, Sunflowers is proof that beauty can endure. It is a testament to humanity's ability to preserve, to hope, and to believe in something greater than ourselves. It is, as Vincent hoped, a beacon for those who need light in their darkness.*

HANA LEANED back in her chair, rereading her words. She thought about her own life—the moments she had doubted herself, the times when the weight of her work felt overwhelming. Yet, in uncovering the story of Sunflowers, she had found her own connection to its message.

The painting wasn't just about light or beauty. It was about resilience, about the universal search for meaning in a world that so often feels chaotic.

She typed her final lines:

*As I stand before Sunflowers, I see more than paint and canvas. I see lives intertwined, stories woven together by a common thread. I see a field of gold that stretches beyond time, carrying with it the hope and humanity of those who came before us.*

*And I am reminded that, like the sunflowers themselves, we too can turn toward the light.*

Hana saved the document, her chest lighter than it had felt in weeks. She closed her laptop and looked out the window, where the late afternoon sun bathed the city in a warm glow.

Outside, life continued—people walking, cars passing, the buzz of the world carrying on. Yet, in her heart, she felt a quiet connection to something eternal.

The field of gold was still there, waiting to be seen, waiting to remind anyone who looked that there is always light, even in the darkness.

# AFTERWORD

Vincent van Gogh was a man of profound contradictions—a restless, brilliant soul who lived on the edge of despair and hope. Born in 1853 in Zundert, the Netherlands, he spent much of his early life searching for purpose, dabbling in various professions before committing himself to art at the age of 27. His journey as an artist was marked by relentless self-doubt, financial hardship, and an overwhelming desire to connect with the world through his work.

### Struggles

Vincent's struggles were many, and they shaped every brush-stroke he placed on canvas. At the core of his pain was a deep sense of isolation. He often felt misunderstood, even by those closest to him. His turbulent relationship with his father, the rejection of his romantic advances, and the indifference of the art world left him feeling like an outsider. His letters to his brother Theo, his closest confidant, reveal the depths of his loneliness and the rawness of his emotional battles.

His mental health further compounded his struggles. Vincent experienced episodes of intense depression, anxiety, and psychosis, which eventually led to his confinement in asylums.

The infamous incident of cutting off part of his ear during a breakdown is emblematic of the turmoil that plagued him. Though he sought help and tried to stabilize himself, his erratic mental state made life a constant battle between his inner demons and his desire to create.

Financial hardship also haunted Vincent. He relied heavily on Theo's support, which was both a blessing and a burden. He longed to prove himself in the art world, but during his lifetime, his works were largely dismissed. The rejection gnawed at his fragile self-esteem, leaving him questioning whether his vision had value.

**Hopes**

Despite these immense challenges, Vincent's art was an unrelenting act of hope. Every canvas he painted was an attempt to find beauty and meaning in a world that often felt cruel and indifferent. His obsession with capturing light—whether it was the flickering glow of a café at night, the soft hues of a wheat field, or the golden brilliance of sunflowers—was a reflection of his yearning for something transcendent.

For Vincent, Sunflowers symbolized much of what he hoped to achieve. He saw the flowers as more than just decorative objects; they were alive, vibrant, reaching toward the sun with an energy he both admired and craved. He painted them as a gift to his friend Paul Gauguin, imagining that they would adorn the walls of their "Studio of the South," a haven for artistic collaboration. The series was meant to convey friendship, warmth, and the resilience of life—a testament to his belief in art as a form of connection.

Vincent's hopes extended beyond personal recognition. In his letters, he often expressed a longing for his work to bring solace to others, to be a light in their darkness. He believed that beauty had the power to heal, that even in decay, there was something eternal and redemptive. He dreamed that one day, long after he was gone, his art might be understood and appreciated for the honesty and humanity it conveyed.

### Legacy of Struggles and Hopes

Though Vincent died in 1890, believing himself a failure, his struggles and hopes have become the very essence of his legacy. His work, once dismissed, is now celebrated as a profound expression of the human condition. The very qualities that made him an outcast in his time—his vulnerability, his unorthodox style, his emotional intensity—are now what draw people to his art.

Sunflowers, in particular, stands as a beacon of his enduring hope. Its golden hues, bold strokes, and celebration of light remind viewers of the beauty that can emerge from struggle. In many ways, Vincent's work transcends his own life, offering solace and inspiration to those who, like him, wrestle with their own darkness while yearning for light.

Through his art, Vincent's voice endures, reminding the world that even in its most fragile moments, humanity has the power to create something timeless, something filled with hope.

# AUTHOR'S NOTE

*D*ear Reader,

Thank you for picking up *Vincent's Sunflowers: A Tale of Love, Light and Legacy*. This story began as a simple fascination with Vincent van Gogh's Sunflowers, one of the most celebrated paintings in art history. Like so many, I was captivated by its bold, golden hues and the raw emotion in every brushstroke. But as I delved deeper into its history, I found myself drawn to something even more profound—the lives it has touched, the journeys it has taken, and the enduring hope it symbolizes.

Vincent van Gogh created Sunflowers not only as a work of art but as a message to the world. Through his struggles and isolation, he painted light into life, believing that beauty could bring joy to others, even long after he was gone. This story honors that belief, exploring the threads of humanity that have been woven into the painting's journey across time.

From the quiet resilience of Jakob Rosenfeld, who hid the painting during the terrors of World War II, to the strength of Akiko Takahashi, who found solace in its golden blooms during Japan's recovery, to Hana Mori's modern quest to uncover its story, Sunflowers stands as a testament to the power of art to connect us across generations and continents.

As I wrote this book, I was reminded of the ways art illuminates the human spirit, even in the darkest moments. It speaks to our shared struggles, our dreams, and our capacity to endure. My hope is that this story inspires you to look for the light in your own life and to recognize the beauty in both the fragility and strength of humanity.

Thank you for embarking on this journey with me. I hope *Vincent's Sunflowers* stays with you, not just as a story, but as a reminder that even in moments of shadow, there is always light to be found.

Warmly,

Cassandra

xx

# EXCERPT WHERE IS
# SALVATOR MUNDI

# PREFACE

Where is Leonardo da Vinci's portrait of Salvator Mundi?

Has the world's most expensive painting ever sold, da Vinci's portrait of Christ—the savior of the world, been stolen?

In this fictional tale, bestselling author and award-winning artist, Cassandra Gaisford answers these questions and raises a tantalizing premise. What if the world's greatest art heist is a deliberate ploy to deceive the world?

Art crime? Money laundering? Political ruse? Or the greatest gamble of the century?

Turn the pages and discover for yourself.

# PROLOGUE

*A*rt crime expert, Noor Charming, was perplexed. The answer to the world's most glamorous mystery was obvious to those with eyes to see and ears to hear. As Leonardo once said, 'the truth is best hidden in plain sight.'

But nobody could see, nobody could hear, nobody could believe what Noor knew so clearly.

It's a ruse. A game. They are playing a hoax. Driving the international art cavalry wild with their immature game of hide and seek.

They are laughing, laughing all the way to the Saudi bank. The longer the painting stays missing the greater the speculation and the more priceless the painting will become.

They want *Salvator Mundi* to surpass the *Mona Lisa* in its international infamy.

Welcome to the world of art.

They had mastered the art of deception.

Noor knew all too well that the history of painting was packed with true-crime stories—both fictional and true—all fascinating, illuminating and often bizarre.

She knew many brilliant and powerful minds were driven by an intriguing mixture of genius, pride, revenge, fame, crime, opportunism, money and power.

What she didn't know was, where was Leonardo's portrait of Salvator Mundi and when would it be rediscovered?

# 1

---

"**W**hy is she so famous? A woman! Her portrait cannot be more famous than a man—*than Christ!*" spat Saudi Crown Prince Mohammed bin Salman.

Bader bin Abdullah bin Mohammed bin Farhan al-Saud, a little-known Saudi prince, with no interest in art whatsoever, sat silently. He had done the Prince's bidding. He had purchased the painting on his behalf.

He knew what to do now.

Shut his mouth.

And so he listened…

"SHE IS the face of the whore. His is the savior. It is not Christ that Leonardo has painted it is Mohammed.

His true self masked by the American woman who restored, or rather rewrote, his face. His story.

Yet the truth remains. His knowing eyes, the crystal ball, that sees all.

## 2

---

*L*eonardo was inspired by Islam. The world needs to know that. They need to heed that.

Did you know his mother, Caterina, was Arabic?

Leonardo was not a man of the West, nor corrupted by the French who have betrayed the Islamic world. Leonardo was a man of the Middle East. He painted his Truth.

*Our Truth.*

Yes, we paid a fortune. Why not? It's only play money anyway. The deal was a masterstroke. Let's just say Christie's did very well out of the sale—as they have all our transactions.

Vast fortunes bounce from here to there and then to who knows where. Did I tell you? I recently purchased a palace in France, another in Russia— not even a slip of paper signed. Nothing to link me. I have our allies, Trump and Putin, to thank for that. So clever. No one can pin a thing on Trump—not even taxes. Ha! Ha!

## 3

*A*ll I had to do was help my Russian friend. Buy his painting and pay an extraordinarily stratospheric price. What I really got is a painting, and a yacht, and a palace, and women. Yes, women.

So many women. I tire of them. It's like eating too much chocolate or drinking too much wine only sickly and more treacherous.

No, no, no. The Louvre's femme fatale, the *Mona Lisa*, cannot prevail. Our clever ruse will be her death knell. We shall learn from her, study her, replicate and retell our story until she is no longer of interest.

We have hidden *Salvador Mundi*, just like, in 1911, that Italian handyman did when he whipped the Mona Lisa off the wall of the Louvre.

A brazen act they said. Not as audacious as my 'robbery'. Taken in plain sight marinated in a blaze of publicity and flashing iPhones.

Fools that they are, distracted by their selfies—they never suspected a thing.

The world's greatest art heist was streamed live to the world.


DID YOU ENJOY THIS EXCERPT?
Available now.

.

# AFTERWORD

# AUTHOR'S NOTE

If you have anything to add I certainly welcome all comments.

Thanks for your interest

Much love

Cassandra

# ABOUT THE AUTHOR

Cassandra Gaisford is an internationally acclaimed, award-winning author and artist celebrated for her ability to weave art, history, and emotion into her captivating novels. With a background in psychology, interior architecture and a deep passion for painting, Cassandra brings the world of art to life on the page, blending meticulous research with her personal creative experiences.

Her art-related novels invite readers to explore the transformative power of creativity, often delving into the lives of iconic artists or the hidden stories behind their works. Fans of her fiction praise her for richly textured narratives, vibrant characters, and her talent for transporting readers to breathtakingly vivid settings, from Renaissance ateliers to modern-day art studios.

Drawing inspiration from her own career as an artist, as well as the works of visionaries like Vincent van Gogh, Mark Rothko, and Sarah Dunant, Cassandra's stories resonate with authenticity and heart. Whether unraveling a mystery within a masterpiece or portraying the struggles and triumphs of a creative soul, Cassandra's books offer a celebration of resilience, passion, and the indelible human spirit.

When not writing or painting, Cassandra can be found drawing inspiration from her garden or sharing her joy for creativity in workshops and retreats. Her books, like her art, are a testament to the belief that imagination and courage can transform lives.

She is currently working on a novel of art-related historical and modern fiction inspired by Leonardo da Vinci's portrait, *The Mona Lisa.*

# PLEASE LEAVE A REVIEW

Word of mouth is the most powerful marketing force in the universe. If you found this book useful, I'd appreciate you rating this book and leaving a review. You don't have to say much—just a few words about how the book helped you learn something new or made you feel.

Reviews also help me out a lot in rankings and allows me to do what I love full time.

Thank you so much! I appreciate you!

PS: If you enjoyed this book, do me a small favor to help spread the word about it and share on Facebook, Twitter and other social networks.

# STAY IN TOUCH

**Continue To Be Supported, Encouraged, and Inspired**

www.thejoyfulartist.co.nz
https://www.facebook.com/CGTheJoyfulArtist/
https://www.instagram.com/the_joyful_artiste/
www.youtube.com/cassandragaisfordnz
https://www.thejoyfulartist.co.nz/category/blog/
https://www.thejoyfulartist.co.nz/book-collections/
www.tiktok.com/@cassandrathejoyfulartist

**NEWSLETTERS**

For inspiring tools and helpful tips, subscribe to Cassandra's free newsletters. **Sign up now and receive a free eBook —find your passion and purpose!** http://eepurl.com/bEArfT

Follow me on BookBub (https://www.bookbub.com/profile/cassandra-gaisford) and be the first to know about my new releases and giveaways

# COVER IMAGE CREDIT

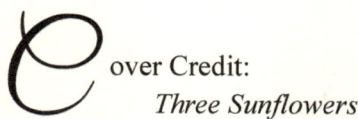

over Credit:
*Three Sunflowers*

This is the mysterious so-called "Lausanne" *Sunflowers*. It was purchased by an unidentified private collector from a New York dealer in 1996 for an undisclosed sum. The last time it was exhibited was in 1948 when the Cleveland had it for a month. Previously it had been exhibited three times for a total of just six weeks in Paris. Since the 1948 exhibition its movements have been shrouded in mystery and few people have seen it in recent years. The painting is said to be in excellent condition. This image, from Martin Bailey's 2013 book, is likely the best image available, Bailey doesn't give a picture credit.

1888
**Medium**
oil on canvas
**Dimensions**
height: 73 cm (28.7 in); width: 58 cm (22.8 in)

**Collection**
Private collection
**Place of creation**
Arles

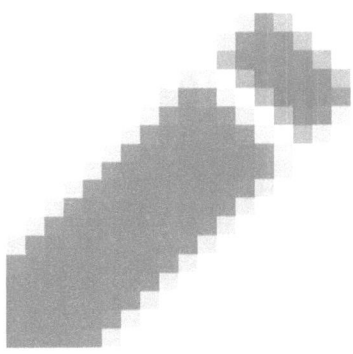

SOURCE: WikiCommons

# COPYRIGHT FICTION

www.Cassandragaisford.com